MY RIVER

by Shari Halpern

SCHOLASTIC INC.

New York Toronto London Auckland Sydney

For their help with this book, I would like to thank John Cronin, Alan Reingold, Judy Sue Goodwin-Sturges, Beverly Reingold, Jean Krulis, James P. Rod, and Lynne O'Malley.

For specific information about how to help our rivers, contact:
Riverkeeper, P.O. Box 130, Garrison, NY 10524.

Copyright © 1992 by Shari Halpern.
All rights reserved. Published by Scholastic Inc., 730 Broadway,
New York, NY 10003, by arrangement with Macmillan Publishing Company.
Printed in the U.S.A.
The text of this book is set in 36 pt. Mixage Medium.
The illustrations are rendered in collage.

ISBN 0-590-47237-2
ISBN 0-590-29051-7 (meets NASTA specifications)

5 6 7 8 9 10   24   00 99 98 97 96

For Maw, Pop, and Maura,
who are pleased and proud

and for Jaclyn,
who would have been

Whose river is this?

It's my river.

It's our river.

9

It's everyone's river!

This is my home.

We live here, too.

I was born here.

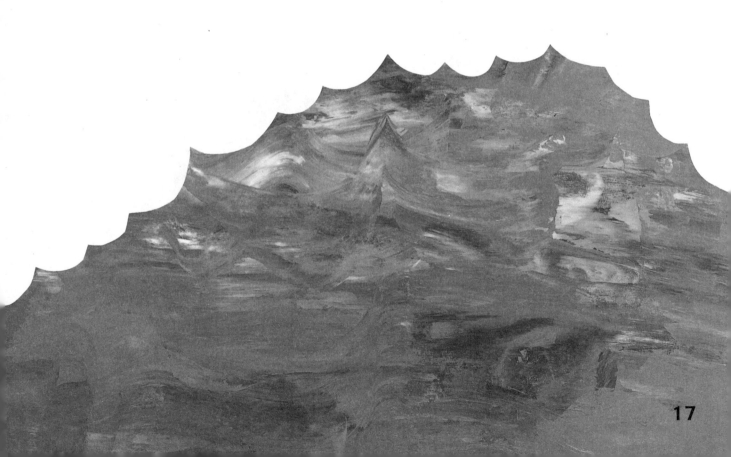

This is where we grow.

19

I need the river.

So do we.

We *all* need the river!

This river is mine.

27

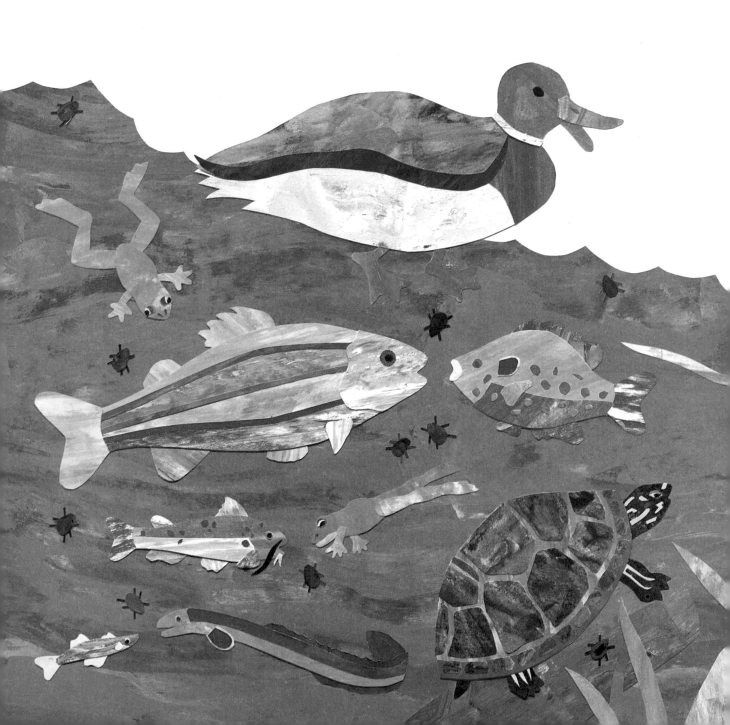

Whose river is it?

It's *everyone's* river!

 turtle

 vegetation

 frog

 muskrat

 fish

 water beetle

 eel

 duck

 salamander

 crayfish

 dragonfly

 children